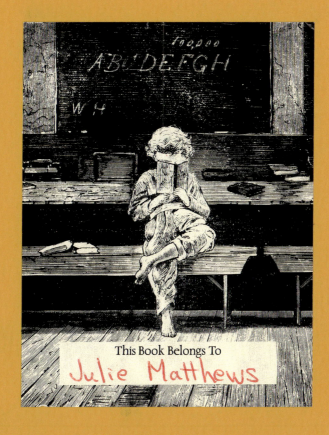

This Book Belongs To

Julie Matthews

MARGARET & TAYLOR

written and illustrated by

KEVIN HENKES

GREENWILLOW BOOKS
New York

Library of Congress Cataloging in Publication Data

Henkes, Kevin.   Margaret & Taylor.
Summary: Relates several short episodes of Margaret and her
brother Taylor, all pertaining to Grandpa's surprise birthday party.
[1. Brothers and sisters—Fiction.   2. Parties— Fiction]
I. Title.   II. Title: Margaret and Taylor.
PZ7.H389Mar 1983   [E]   82-21134
ISBN 0-688-01425-9
ISBN 0-688-01426-7 (lib. ed.)

For Peter, Jon, Peggy & Chris
again & again
on & on . . .

CONTENTS

1

THE INVITATION

Taylor always waited for Barney, the mailman. Taylor usually didn't get any mail, but he liked to sit and wait and think of all the things that might come.

That particular day, there were three long envelopes, two fat envelopes and a small blue envelope.

"Nothing for you, Taylor," said Barney, "except this one. It says 'The Tippet Family.' So at least part of it is for you."

It was the small blue envelope. And it smelled like perfume. Taylor sniffed the envelope and wondered what could be in it.

"Did we get any mail?" asked his sister Margaret. "Let me see those," she said, grabbing the envelopes. "This one smells pretty."

"Maybe there's a flower inside," said Taylor.

"It's too flat," said Margaret.

"Maybe a skinny flower," said Taylor. "Or a tiny one."

"No, no, no," said Margaret. "But why don't you open it up? Then we'll know for sure."

"Shouldn't we wait for Mother to get back from the store?" asked Taylor.

"I don't think so," said Margaret. "The envelope says 'The Tippet Family.' And you're part of this family."

"You are too," said Taylor, "so you should help."

"Okay, we'll each do half," said Margaret. "You can go first."

"Why?" asked Taylor.

"Because," said Margaret, "you saw it first. And you're the one who *really* wants to find out what's inside."

Taylor took the envelope from Margaret.

"Are you sure I should do this?" he asked.

"Of course," said Margaret.

Taylor started ripping the envelope. He did his half and looked at Margaret.

"There, now it's your turn," he said, handing her the envelope.

"You have to do a little more," said Margaret.

"Are you sure?" asked Taylor.

"Of course," said Margaret.

Taylor opened the envelope a tiny bit more. He looked up at Margaret.

"A little, little more," she said.

Through the window, Margaret saw Mother coming up the driveway.

"Keep going," she said to Taylor.

When Mother came in, Margaret said, "Look at Taylor, he's opening the mail."

Mother took the envelope and opened it all the way.

"It's an invitation from Grandma," said Mother. "She's having a surprise party for Grandpa's birthday."

"When?" asked Taylor. "What should we get Grandpa? Will we have a cake?"

Before Mother could answer, Margaret said, "But, Mother, what about Taylor? He was opening the envelope."

Mother smiled. "Sometimes," she said, "surprises just won't wait."

THE PRESENT

16

Margaret and Taylor were walking to the store. It was the day of Grandpa's party and they needed a present.

Margaret walked fast. Taylor walked slow. He collected leaves and counted the rocks.

"Hurry up!" said Margaret.

"Let's look for a present in the toy department," said Margaret.

"Would Grandpa *want* a toy?" asked Taylor.

"Of course," said Margaret. "And that way we'll have something new to play with."

Margaret saw a stuffed elephant. It was in a box covered with cellophane. The box said SOFTEST TOY EVER!

Margaret wanted to touch the elephant to make sure, so she punched her finger through the wrapping. Taylor wanted to try it, and just as he was about to, Margaret grabbed his hand.

"No," she said. "Remember, we're here to buy a present for Grandpa."

Margaret led Taylor to the furniture department.

"Grandpa's chairs are all too hard," said Margaret. "I think he needs a soft one."

"Do we have enough money for a chair?" asked Taylor.

Margaret didn't answer. She was already sitting on a chair, testing it.

Margaret moved back and forth. She bounced up and down.

"That looks like fun," said Taylor, as he

climbed onto a chair of his own.

"Get down from there," said Margaret. She pulled Taylor's leg. "Come on, we're here to buy a present for Grandpa."

"Grandpa could use a new hat," said Margaret. "His is old and gray."

"I like it," said Taylor. "So does Grandpa. He wears it all the time."

"But look at those," said Margaret, pointing. "They have feathers and birds and bows on them."

"Grandpa would look funny with feathers and birds and bows on his head," said Taylor.

But Margaret wasn't listening. She was trying on the hat with feathers. She tried on the hat with birds. She tried on the hat with bows.

Taylor picked up one of the hats.

Margaret looked at him.

"There isn't time for you to try on hats," she said. "Did you forget? We're here to buy a present for Grandpa."

But it was getting late. It was almost time for the party to start. Margaret and Taylor had to go.

As they left, Margaret said, "Just because of your playing around, we have nothing for Grandpa. You didn't remember."

Taylor nodded. He pulled his hand from behind his back.

"Oh, yes, I did," he said. "*I* remembered. I remembered all the time."

THE PARTY

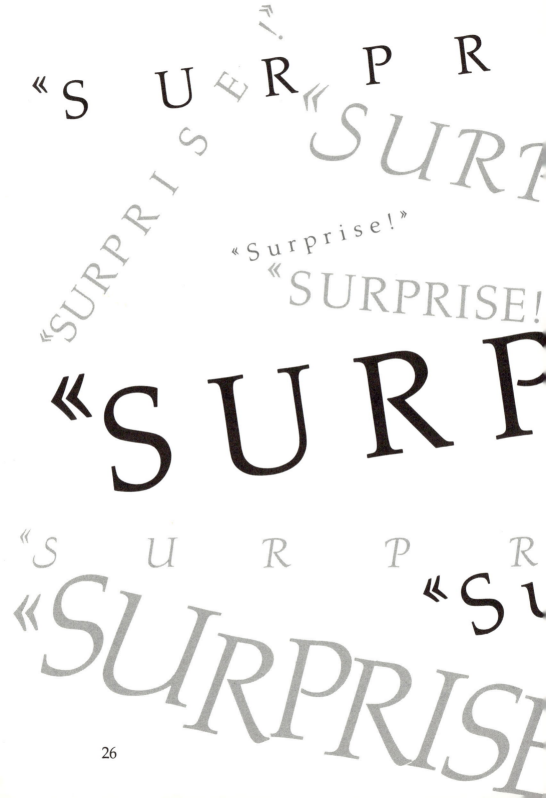

«S U R P R I

«SURPRISE!»

«SURPRISE!»

«Surprise!»

«SURPRISE!»

«SURP

«S U R P R

«Su

«SURPRISE

27

THE BALLOONS

*A*fter they got home from Grandpa's, Margaret and Taylor sat on the front porch before going to bed.

They were holding their balloons from the party. Margaret's was yellow with orange stripes. Taylor's was red all over.

The wind was blowing, so the balloons bobbed up and down.

"Look!" said Taylor. "Mine's a giant floating tomato."

Margaret didn't look. She was tying the string from her balloon to her wrist.

"See?" she said. "Now my balloon is safe. It can't blow away."

"Will you help me do mine?" asked Taylor.

"You're big enough to tie
by yourself," said Margaret.
"Don't be a baby."

Taylor looped the string around his wrist.
When the wind gusted again, his balloon sailed
away.

"Help!" yelled Taylor. "Come back!"

But it was too late. His balloon was gone.

"Too bad," said Margaret. "I was just thinking of all the things we could do with our balloons. We could draw ugly faces on them and then walk under windows, so the faces would scare the people inside."

Taylor tried not to listen.

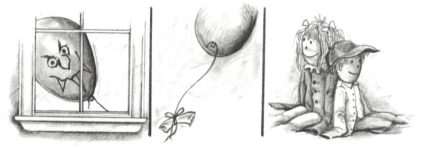

"Or," said Margaret, "we could write secret messages and sign our names and address, tie them to the balloons, and send them off. Then we'd get mail from faraway places."

The more Margaret talked, the worse Taylor felt.

"Or," said Margaret, "we could pretend the balloons were real people—brother and sister. We could use yarn for hair and dress them in old clothes.

"But now *you* can't," said Margaret. "You should be more careful."

Taylor didn't say anything. He just looked at Margaret's balloon.

From inside the house, Father called, "Time for bed, you two."

Margaret untied her balloon on the way in.

"See?" she said. "Even untied, if you're *very* careful and hold on tight, nothing can happen."

When Margaret opened the door, their dog Chopper jumped up on her.

"Look out!" cried Margaret. But her balloon

got away. Margaret ran down the steps after it, but it was too high and too far away to catch. She watched her balloon until she couldn't see it any longer. Then Margaret yelled at Chopper and ran inside the house.

"It's okay," said Taylor, petting Chopper. "Maybe the balloons really were brother and sister. And now they can be together."

5

THE CAKE

Margaret saved a piece of cake from Grand-pa's party. She put it under her bed and took it out the next morning for breakfast.

In the kitchen, Taylor was already eating his oatmeal. But when he saw Margaret's cake, he wanted it.

"It's mine," said Margaret. "You had yours last night."

"But I just had a little piece," said Taylor, "not half as big as that. And you had some too!"

"Did I?" said Margaret. "Why don't you pretend that your oatmeal is birthday cake? The oatmeal can be the chocolate part. The milk can be the frosting. The sugar can be the squiggles. And you can imagine all the yellow roses."

Taylor added lots of frosting.

He put on lots of squiggles.

He imagined lots of yellow roses.

Then he took a taste and thought hard. But no matter how hard he tried, his oatmeal just tasted like oatmeal.

Margaret looked at the cake. She looked at Taylor looking at the cake.

"I'll make a deal," she said, smiling. "I'll give you a piece if you give me your dessert at dinner tonight."

Taylor looked at the cake. He looked at the oatmeal. He tasted the oatmeal again. It was cold, so he said, "Yes!"

"I have to be fair," said Margaret. "Your

piece should fit your size."

First she cut the cake in half. She cut it in half again. Then she took one of the small pieces and cut it once more.

"Here," she said, "this looks like your size."

Margaret set the piece of cake next to Taylor.

Taylor looked at the cake. It looked more like a crumb. There wasn't much frosting. There were no yellow roses.

Just then the phone rang. It was Margaret's friend Dodie, asking her to go swimming.

Margaret ran upstairs to ask Mother. She changed into her swimsuit and ran out the door.

She didn't even say good-bye to Taylor.

Margaret forgot about the cake.

But Taylor didn't.

6

THE HAT

Margaret took her hat from Grandpa's party and tied a string to its tassel. Then she took her gum and stuck it to the other end of the string. She climbed up her dresser and stuck the gum to the ceiling. The hat dangled down.

"What is that?" asked Taylor.

"This is my friend Lillian," said Margaret. "She was at Grandpa's party, but you couldn't see her. She's invisible most of the time."

"Can you see her?" asked Taylor.

"Of course," said Margaret.

"I can see her hat," said Taylor.

"That's because I told her to show it to you," said Margaret. "But I bet you can't see her long curly hair or her diamond rings or her purple shoes."

"Tell her to show me her purple shoes," said Taylor. "Please?"

"Lillian says she'll show her purple shoes if you make my bed for me," said Margaret.

So Taylor made Margaret's bed.

"I still don't see the purple shoes," said Taylor.

"Lillian says she'll show you her purple shoes if you promise to help Daddy with the dishes tonight, instead of me," said Margaret.

"I promise," he said, crossing his heart.

"I *still* don't see the purple shoes," said Taylor.

"Lillian says she'll show you her purple shoes if you sit in here alone and talk to her awhile," said Margaret.

"Okay," said Taylor.

So Margaret went outside to play and left Taylor with Lillian.

"I'm four," said Taylor. "How old are you?"

There was no answer.

"I like baseball and rockets and bottlecaps," said Taylor. "What do you like?"

There was still no answer.

Suddenly the hat fell down. And Taylor saw the string and the gum just lying there. Lillian was gone.

So Taylor took the hat and the string, and the gum he was chewing, and climbed up his dresser. He stuck the string to the ceiling in his room.

Then he went outside to look for his friend Phil.

"Phil!" he said. "Come over to my house and see my invisible friend."

THE BEST SURPRISE

Margaret and Taylor were drawing pictures. Margaret's picture was of a sunflower. Taylor's was of Grandpa at his party.

"Your picture is nice," said Taylor.

"Of course," said Margaret. "It's a sunflower. What is yours supposed to be?"

"It's Grandpa at his party," said Taylor.

"It doesn't look like Grandpa," said Margaret.

"Yes, it does," said Taylor.

Margaret turned Taylor's picture upside down.

"It still doesn't look like Grandpa," she said.

Margaret turned Taylor's picture sideways.

"It *still* doesn't look like Grandpa," said Margaret. "But I can fix it."

"No!" said Taylor. "It's mine and I like it the way it is. Grandpa would like it too."

"Grandpa wouldn't even know it was him," said Margaret.

Margaret tried to take the drawing away from Taylor. But he wouldn't let go. Just when it was about to rip, there was a knock on the window.

"What was that?" asked Taylor.

"Maybe," said Margaret, "it's a giant sun-flower coming to fix your picture." She was laughing.

They ran out to the porch. It was Grandpa.

"Grandpa!" said Taylor.

"Grandpa!" said Margaret.

"I came to thank my two favorites for coming to my party and surprising me," said Grandpa. "And now, I have a Grandpa surprise for you."

Margaret and Taylor knew what it was. It was a game they always played with Grandpa.

Grandpa took his hands from his pockets. His fists were closed.

"One is for Margaret," said Grandpa, "and one is for Taylor."

Margaret grabbed his right fist and opened it up.

"There's nothing here," she said, smiling.

Taylor grabbed his left fist and opened it up.

"There's nothing here, either," he said, giggling.

"I know," said Grandpa, "and that's so I can hug you both at the very same time."

Grandpa loved Margaret's picture of the sunflower.

And he knew right away Taylor's picture was of him.